Scott & Ralphie Sam hi!

Chane

Join the adventure and join the fun!

Order Today!
www.pinkyandpeanut.com

Here's what people are saying about the Pinky and Peanut series:

Meet two independent girls who will make you laugh as they juggle friendship, family, and school. Even their names Pinky and Peanut shout out their individuality.

—Mary C.

As a teacher and parent of two (a son and daughter), I highly recommend the Pinky and Peanut series to any parent who wants to teach their children valuable life lessons through these great stories and fun characters!

—Brian F.

I love Pinky and Peanut because it is like my life. There is a dog and I love dogs. It's a fun book with lots of friends. It's so fun to read.

—Ivy, Age 9

Another fun, exciting book for emerging readers. Another favorite for all 3 of my kids!! Waiting for the saga to continue....brings back fond memories of my own childhood.

—Karen C.

I like Pinky and Peanut because I could not put the book down. I wanted to keep reading it and reading it! I love their adventures. I hope there are more. I can't wait for the next book.

—Hanley, age 7

As with the first book in this series, my grandchildren just loved this book. They read it over and over. They'll probably read it years from now just for the memories.

—Roger B.

Pinky and Peanut

Book Three

No Boys Allowed

Pinky and Peanut

Book Three

No Boys Allowed

BY
Deena Cook
AND
Cherie McIntosh

ILLUSTRATIONS BY Trina Scruggs

P&P Publishing LLC
Bellevue, WA

Editor: Julie Scandora
Typographer: Stephanie Martindale

For Ethan and all the support you show me each day. It means so much. -Deena

To Michael and my children-my true treasures in life. -Cherie

Acknowledgements

To our parents. We couldn't have gone on this adventure without you.
To our readers. You have blessed our jobs with your enthusiasm and love of reading.

Contents

No Boys Allowed

Prologue

Both Pinky and Peanut had moved to Oakdale the summer before second grade. Each thought that moving would ruin their lives forever, but luckily for the girls, they had moved in right across the street from each other. They became the best of friends. To make it even better, Peanut had found a hidden clubhouse in her backyard. They spent the rest of the summer playing, writing in their special journal, and hanging out with Peanut's dog, Ralphie. The only thing that drove them kind of crazy was Peanut's brother Scott. He liked to bug and tease them whenever he could. But the girls didn't let that bother them … too much.

Chapter 1

What Was That?

"We're so lucky we got the new *Super Samantha* comic book before they ran out at the store," Peanut said, turning the pages.

"I can't believe they sold out in one day," Pinky answered back, "and we had to wait in line for a whole hour. That was so crazy."

❖❖❖❖❖❖❖

Lots of children at Oakdale Elementary loved the *Super Samantha* series about a girl who saves the world with her best friend, Amazing Jake. The super heroes had even visited the shopping mall two towns away. The girls had

gotten their autographs and a picture taken with Super Samantha that they proudly displayed in the clubhouse. Although the girls couldn't understand why anyone would want to have a boy for a best friend, they still loved the stories and eagerly waited for each new book.

Pinky and Peanut were spending a quiet, rainy Saturday afternoon in their clubhouse. They were taking turns drawing pictures of themselves with Super Samantha in their journal. Ralphie, Peanut's dog, was lying on his favorite doggie bed in the corner of the clubhouse, chewing on a bone.

"If you could have any super power in the world, Peanut, what would it be?"

"I would want to fly. We would never have to take the bus again. We could fly to any park we wanted. And we could even fly to our favorite ice cream store."

"YES!" they said at the exact same time.

"What would you want to have, Pinky?"

"That's easy, Peanut. I would be Super-fast Girl!"

"Why would you want to be super fast?"

"Well, because, I could get all my chores done, do my homework, eat my dinner, and be at the clubhouse in one minute."

"Oh, Pinky, I want that one too," giggled Peanut.

"Okay, we can both have it."

"Hey, what about if Ralphie could fly?"

Ralphie picked up his head, tilted it to the side, and went back to chewing on his bone.

This made both girls laugh until their stomachs hurt.

Still giggling, Peanut said, "We better get back to drawing so we can finish our picture before dinner."

"*Ping, ping.*"

"Peanut, what was that?" Pinky asked, jumping up from the floor.

"Pinky, you are so funny. I'm sure it was nothing."

"You're right," she said, sitting back down on the floor. "*Ping, ping.*"

"Okay, now I definitely heard that," Pinky said, jumping up again.

"Me, too!"

"What do you think it is?"

"I'm not sure, but let's go find out," Peanut said, putting on her bravest smile.

"Are you sure we should peek?" Pinky asked nervously.

"Umm, yes."

"Okay, we'll open the door on the count of three. One, two ..."

Before the girls could say three, the door flew open, and Scott yelled "BOO!" making both girls scream loudly.

"Ha, ha! Fooled you again," he said with a smirky smile. "When will you guys ever stop screaming like babies?"

"Get out of here, Scott!" Pinky yelled.

"Yeah, Scott ... out!" shouted Peanut.

"Better watch out, you two," he said with a laugh. "Things are about to get a lot more fun in Oakdale."

The girls hated Scott always ruining their fun, but this time, his words made them feel a bit scared. What did he mean? They watched him from the clubhouse window as he ran back to the house. Mac and Ethan (Scott's two best friends) were sitting on the back porch with a few other boys, waiting for a game of touch football to begin.

"I wish Scott would find another yard to play football in." Peanut said, rolling her eyes at her best friend.

"Well, he has to have some place to play since we have the clubhouse, right?" Pinky stated.

"I know, I know."

Pinky and Peanut just looked at each other. What could they say? With the way Scott had just acted, he was up to something, and it made both girls nervous.

Chapter 2

Calling All Super Heroes

"Peanut, I really want to know what Scott meant when he said that we better watch out. I don't feel so good about this," Pinky said as she stared out the window of their school bus.

"Oh, Pinky, I'm sure Scott was just messing around. You know how he always teases us."

Peanut's words make her sound braver than she felt. This time, Scott wasn't just bugging them; he seemed different. Was he planning something? What was he up to?

"You're right," Pinky said, giving her a hug.

"Hey," Peanut said, trying to change the subject, "did you see what was on the back of the new comic book?"

Peanut pulled out her *Super Samantha* comic book and opened to the back page. There in large, bright, green letters it read:

Calling All Super Heroes!
Have you ever wished you had
super powers? If so, write us
and tell us your story. If you
are picked, Super Samantha and
Amazing Jake will visit your school
as your special guests.
Enter Today!!!!

"Do you think she'd really come to our school? Do you really think we'd have a chance?"

"Well, it doesn't say people from Oakdale can't enter. Right, Pinky? We have as good a chance as anyone."

"Okay, Peanut. Let's do this."

"Do what?" Scott said leaning over the bus seat.

"Wouldn't you like to know, Scott?" Pinky said.

Before the girls could react, Scott reached over the seat and ripped the comic book out of Peanut's hand.

"Hey!!!" both girls yelled at the same time.

"Ooooh," Scott said in a loud voice, making sure everyone on the bus could hear. "It's Super Samantha. Everyone knows that Amazing Jake is the coolest one anyway."

Pinky and Peanut could hear kids all over the bus laughing. Why did everyone think Scott was so funny?

"A contest?" Scott said, turning around, looking at the girls.

"You don't really think you can win this, do you?" Scott flopped down onto his seat, laughing. "You two don't have a chance."

"Scott, cool it!" said their older brother, Paul. "Leave the girls alone. Why are you always making trouble for them?"

Paul took the comic book out of Scott's hands and handed it back to Peanut.

"Here you go, Peanut."

"I'm soooo lucky to have a niiicccce brother," Peanut said while glaring at Scott.

"Why can't Scott ever leave us alone?" Pinky said, rolling her eyes and folding her arms.

"Just think; I have to live with him everyday. At least your twin brothers are still too small to talk."

As the bus pulled into Oakdale Elementary, the girls couldn't wait to race off the bus and get as far away as they could from Scott. They made a quick dash over to their friend Tammy to tell her about the contest. No way would they let Scott ruin their day.

Chapter 3

Ideas, Plans, and Scott. Oh My!

"Walk, girls," Principal McPatrick said with a smile. Ever since Super Samantha and Amazing Jake had visited the local mall, the students had too much excited energy, and he was constantly reminding them to lower their voices or stop running in the hall. He couldn't be too mad, though; he liked seeing all the smiles.

"Sorry!" all the girls said, embarrassed.

Hours later, the two girls flopped onto their chairs in the lunchroom, and Pinky exclaimed, "Finally, Peanut!"

"I can't believe that out of all the days we really needed to talk, we couldn't."

"I know," Peanut said. "I was going crazy."

"Can you believe Mrs. Carson kept us busy the whole morning?" said Tammy, sitting down next to the girls.

"All right, we only have twenty minutes. So let's work," Peanut said, taking her journal out of her backpack. "We've got work to do."

"I think we need a plan," Tammy said.

"Here is my idea," said Pinky, leaning over to the girls so only they could hear. "First thing we need to decide is what our super powers will be."

"Good plan, good plan," Tammy and Peanut said at the same time.

"I still want to fly," Peanut blurted out.

She sat for a quick moment, smiling, as she imagined herself flying through the sky.

Tammy and Pinky giggled, just watching her face.

"Tammy, what do you want to be?" asked Pinky. "You weren't at the clubhouse yesterday."

"I want to be invisible."

"Yeah, I thought about that before, too," said Pinky.

"I can pick something different," Tammy quickly answered back.

"No, that's okay; you take it. I totally want to be Super-fast Girl."

"Super-fast Girl?" said Tammy.

"Listen to this, I could get dressed, eat breakfast, brush my teeth, and be on the school bus in one minute. I could sleep in, EVEN on school mornings."

All the girls were excited with the super power they chose. For the next few minutes, they talked and talked about what kind of story they were going to write.

"Okay, it's almost time for recess," said Pinky. "Tonight, we have homework."

"Homework?" said Tammy.

"Not school homework. Superpower homework. When we meet at the clubhouse tomorrow, we need to be ready to tell each other what our super hero name is going to be."

Peanut and Tammy nodded their heads in agreement. Then all three girls stood up, pushed their chairs in, and went out to recess. Sure they could have worked some more, but who wants to miss recess?

<hr>

"Do you think they really have a chance to win this contest?" said Scott, watching the girls run to the playground. "She can't have walkie-talkies, a clubhouse, and win a contest, too. She can't have everything."

"What are you going to do, Scott?" said Ethan.

"I don't know, but give me a little more time. I'll figure it out."

"I know you will," said Mac. "You always do."

The three boys high-fived each other and headed out to play some basketball on the playground.

Chapter 4

Something Strange

"I can't believe I forgot the journal!" Peanut said into the walkie-talkie as she ran into the clubhouse right before bed. Although her mom wasn't too happy about her going to the clubhouse, she gave her a flashlight and watched her from the back porch.

"Why can't you wait until morning?" Pinky answered back into her walkie-talkie.

"Pinky, what if I come up with my superhero name? I would totally lose it if I wrote it on just a piece of paper."

★★★★★★★★

Since moving to Oakdale, Pinky and Peanut had maybe three nights where they hadn't talked to each other on the walkie-talkies before bed. Both of the girls' families didn't understand what they possibly needed to say, especially after having been together most of the day. However, Pinky and Peanut knew there were ALWAYS more things to talk about.

Peanut was just about ready to leave the clubhouse when Pinky heard her say, "Hmm, that's funny?"

"What's funny, Peanut?"

"Oh, um, nothing, Pinky. Hold on and I'll talk to you in a minute when I get back home."

Wasn't the poster on the right side of the door? Peanut stood in the clubhouse with her hands on her hips.

As she walked back to the house, Peanut tried to put the poster out of her mind. *Would Scott be messing with the clubhouse? Why would he go in her clubhouse?*

Calling Pinky back on the walkie-talkie, Peanut told her best friend what she had seen.

"Do you think Scott was in our clubhouse, Peanut?"

"I don't think so, but … oh, Pinky, I don't know."

After saying goodnight, both girls turned off the walkie-talkies and went to bed. But neither girl slept well that night. Scott really was up to something. But what?

Chapter 5

Drum Roll, Please

The next day after school, Pinky, Peanut, and Tammy met at the clubhouse to share their superpower homework. They could hardly keep from blurting out their names at school, but they made it through the whole day. They ran straight to the clubhouse, opened up a package of gummi bears, and flopped on the beanbag chairs.

"Okay, Peanut, since this is your clubhouse, you can go first," said Pinky.

"This is OUR clubhouse … but okay, if you really want me to," said Peanut, smiling.

"The name I chose is Awesome Ashley. What do you think? Do you like it?"

Both Pinky and Tammy gave her two thumbs up.

"That's perfect," said Tammy.

"Thank you very much," replied Awesome Ashley. "Who wants to go next?"

"You go, Tammy," said Pinky.

"You're so cool, Pinky. Thanks a lot."

Tammy cleared her throat, acting as if she was about to give a very important speech. This made everyone giggle.

"My superhero name is going to be Terrific Tammy."

"Perfect!" shouted Peanut.

"Okay, Pinky," Peanut said, "it's your turn. What's your superhero name?"

"Drum roll, please," Pinky began. "I am proud to announce that my name is going to be Super-fast Girl Who Is Quicker Than a Cheetah."

Both Tammy and Peanut looked back and forth at each other, not really sure what to say.

"Do you think that name might be too long?" asked Tammy.

Pinky laughed. "I'm just teasing you guys! I really chose Dynamic Denise!"

"I love it!" said Peanut. "We came up with great names."

"Hey, Pinky, could you go in our art box and bring out the markers? We need to write all the names in the journal."

"You betcha."

Pinky went over to the shelf where they kept their markers. But when she opened up the box, the markers weren't there.

"That's strange," said Pinky.

"What's strange?" asked Peanut.

"The markers aren't here. We always keep them in this box. Peanut, did you take them to the house when you got the journal last night?"

"No."

"This," said Tammy, tapping her chin, "is a mystery."

The girls just looked at each other and didn't know what to say.

Chapter 6

The Mystery

For the next week, every time the girls went to the clubhouse, they noticed things were different. Hadn't they shut the curtains the day before? Was the rug moved over a little bit from its usual spot? Didn't they have the gummi bears by the table and not the window? Who was doing this? And why? This was a mystery the girls weren't sure they wanted to solve.

By Saturday, they had no choice. As Peanut opened the clubhouse door, a poster of a pirate stared at them from the wall.

"That's it!" Peanut shouted. "I knew my brother was up to something."

Scott was lucky that he was sleeping at cousin Jeff's that night. Peanut had a little something to say to her brother. If he thought he could tease her like this, he was wrong.

"Maybe we should talk to your mom, dad, or Paul," Pinky said as she flopped down on the beanbag chair.

"I don't know, Pinky," Peanut said, sitting on the floor. "I don't want to get in trouble again for fighting with Scott. And we can't really prove he did anything …"

The girls didn't have much fun that day in the clubhouse. In fact, they hadn't had a good time the whole week. How were the girls ever going to get their story for the contest written? Ralphie had even stopped coming with them to the clubhouse. It was as if he knew something was up, too.

Chapter 7

Scott!!!

"So, I was thinking about how we should start our story for the contest," Pinky said to Peanut and Tammy a few days later.

It was a sunny day, and the girls had taken sandwiches to the park. They had spent what seemed like hours riding their bikes, playing on the swings, and having the best time. When they were done, they went to the clubhouse for their favorite gummi bear cupcake snack Peanut's mom had made. This day was absolutely the best ever.

"I'm so excited about the contest," Tammy said as she parked her bike in Peanut's driveway.

"So are we!" Pinky and Peanut joined in.

The girls ran across the yard to get to the clubhouse super fast.

Pinky opened the clubhouse door and immediately scared the other two girls. "SCOTT!!!" she screamed.

Peanut and Tammy, who had run smack into Pinky, immediately saw why she had shouted. Sitting on the beanbag chair in the corner of their clubhouse was Scott.

"Hey, girls!" Scott said with a very fake smile on his face. "Whatcha doing? What are we gonna talk about today in our clubhouse?"

The girls stood there with their mouths opened wide. *What did Scott just say? Why was he in their clubhouse?*

"You don't have anything nice to say to your very sweet, funny brother, Peee-nuuut?"

"Oh hello, Scott. What are you doing here?" Tammy said, trying to be polite.

The girls were so happy to have Tammy as a friend. She was always calm when things got crazy.

"Oh hey, Tammy," Scott replied. "I'm just reading my new skateboard magazine in OUR clubhouse, waiting for my friends Mac and Ethan."

"What?" Peanut snapped at Scott, taking a step into the clubhouse.

"Yeah, my club mates," Scott continued very calmly. "We were talking yesterday about a good name for the clubhouse. You don't have one, do you? We do like Skatedudes, but we're okay working with you on a name."

Scott just kept talking on and on, not letting any of the girls speak. "We thought about a club name, what color we'd like to paint the clubhouse, and what kind of things we are going to put on the walls."

Scott would've continued, but Peanut was already racing for the house yelling, "Mom! Dad! Mom! Dad!"

Before Pinky and Tammy could move, Scott ran past them shouting, "I'm gonna get there first, Peanut, and I'll tell them all about …"

The girls couldn't hear what Scott was shouting anymore. All they heard was the back door slamming at Scott and Peanut's house. They looked at each other and knew exactly what the other was thinking: *It couldn't get any worse than this.*

Chapter 8

How Could This Be Happening?

"Mom, Dad, I have something very important to talk to you about," Scott said running into the kitchen.

Peanut tried to give him a dirty look as she ran into the house, but it was too late.

"Great Scott, save it for dinner," Dad said from the family room. "It will be our dinner topic."

If there was one thing Peanut and Scott could agree on, it was that they did NOT want to wait until dinner.

"Can't I just tell you, Dad?" Scott said whining.

"Scott," Mom said, "we will talk about it at dinner."

Every night, they discussed a new topic at the table. Most of the time, the kids didn't mind. However, tonight was going to be very different.

"Scott, set the table," Dad said, handing him the dinner dishes. "Peanut, go work on your homework. Dinner will be in an hour."

It was the longest hour of her life.

"Just be calm Peanut," Pinky had told her on the walkie-talkie five minutes before dinner.

"Listen to your mom and dad. They won't side with him."

Peanut knew her friend was trying to make her feel better. But no matter what Pinky said, it didn't help.

Peanut could hear laughing downstairs. *Scott is telling jokes? Ughhh,* Peanut thought to herself. *What was Scott up to? He was trying to get their parents on his side. Not fair!*

The family had just sat down to dinner, and an anxious Peanut and Scott were ready to the get the meeting started.

"Okay," Dad said, "Scott, you can speak first. What's on your mind?"

Peanut, couldn't believe this! Why did he get to go first? This was not off to a good start.

Peanut stared at Scott, and Scott smirked at Peanut. "Well, I've been looking at the clubhouse everyday while I play outside with my friends," Scott said thoughtfully, "and I have an idea."

Peanut sat up straighter and to hear every word Scott was saying. *Oh no*, she thought, *he's being too sweet. That was never a good sign. Here it comes.* The one thing Pinky and Peanut hoped would never happen was about to come true.

"What's your idea?" Mom replied.

"I'm really glad Peanut and her friends have a place to play. They look like they're always having fun and ..."

Peanut couldn't believe it. Surely her mom and dad wouldn't believe this act Scott was putting on.

"The clubhouse is in my backyard, too. I just think I'd really like to spend some time in it with my friends." Scott then looked at Peanut with the nicest smile he could make.

"NO!" Peanut said, jumping up from her chair.

"Ashley, sit down, please," Mom said in a stern voice. "Your brother has a right to say how he feels, and you need to respect that."

"But, Mom and Dad, the clubhouse is my special place with Pinky. He doesn't even like the clubhouse. He's just trying to make me upset."

"Am not, Peanut," Scott said, interrupting her.

"Scott, this is not fair. You know you're just being mean and trying to make me mad."

"Enough!" Dad said.

"Peanut, I know that you love the clubhouse. I am happy you and Pinky have such a great time there. But, Scott is also right."

Peanut was feeling terrible. She wanted to pretend this wasn't happening. The only problem ... it was!

"We haven't said anything before because Scott has always been okay playing in the yard."

"Dad ...," Peanut said.

"Peanut, wait," Dad said, holding up his hand, letting her know she needed to listen.

"Peanut, we are a family. We all live in this house and share that backyard," he said pointing outside.

"Thank you, Dad," Scott replied.

"Scott, enough already," Mom said with a sigh.

"Okay, listen, you two. Let Mom and me talk about this tonight, and we'll tell you what we have decided in the morning."

"But, Dad ...," both Peanut and Scott said at the same time.

"Kids, that's it. I'll let you know tomorrow. Now eat your dinner, please."

As Peanut finished her meal that evening, she couldn't help but dread the decision her mom and dad would make. Would they take the clubhouse away from her?

What was she going to tell Pinky?

Chapter 9

Waiting

Peanut slowly rolled out of bed. She knew she looked as bad as she felt. With no sleep, it was going to be a very long day. What were Mom and Dad going to tell them? Peanut opened her bedroom door to go brush her teeth when she heard music coming from Scott's room.

Without hesitating, she pounded on his door. "Scott, be quiet in there!"

Scott popped his head out of his room and said, "Make me, Peanut Butter," and slammed the door before she could say anything.

"Scott, you make me so mad!" Peanut screamed.

"Ashley, get down here now!" yelled her mom.

"Here we go," mumbled Peanut.

During breakfast, Mom and Dad told them that they would give them their decision that day.

"What time?" Scott asked.

"When we are ready," Mom replied.

After breakfast, Peanut, Scott, and Paul were sent out to the yard to do their Sunday chores. All the way out, Scott and Peanut argued about anything and everything.

"You know, I'm tired of listening to you two fighting all the time. Give it a rest," Paul said as he stormed off to get the lawn mower.

"What's his problem?" Scott asked.

"I don't know," Peanut answered, shrugging her shoulders.

Peanut hated weeding Mom's flower-beds, not because she had to pull the weeds but because she had to do it with Scott. Today, she had to get as far away from him as possible and started on the opposite side of the yard from him. She needed to think about the contest and her story ideas.

"I just know we are going to win this," she said quietly to herself.

At that exact moment, a clump of weeds hit her on the side of her face. It didn't hurt, but it made her mad.

"Scott, what did you do that for?"

"Do what?"

"You know."

"Why won't they just tell us already?" Scott said, pretending he hadn't just thrown weeds at his sister.

"How would I know?" Peanut said, wiping the rest of the dirt from her cheek. "Maybe they haven't decided yet."

"Yeah," Scott said.

The rest of the morning went by without anymore fighting. Of course, it helped that they didn't talk to each other. But no word from Mom or Dad, either. After Scott and Peanut finished their chores, they stayed away from each other all afternoon.

They couldn't believe that Mom and Dad still hadn't talked to them. Now it was almost time for dinner. Would they finally get their answer?

Chapter 10

The Talk

By dinnertime, all the kids seemed to be fighting about everything.

"Peanut, move your chair over. You're touching mine," Scott whined.

"Am not, Scott!"

"I want the two of you to stay out of my room. Why are you always on my computer?" Paul yelled.

"Enough!" Dad said, coming into the dining room. "I have had it."

Oh no, Peanut thought. When Dad got mad, that was not a good thing at all.

"I expect you to start treating each other with respect. All of you."

"Paul, that includes you. Why are you fighting with your brother and sister?"

"Dad, I'm tired of them always fighting over everything. Plus they were in my room again."

"Is that true?" Mom asked, putting the bowl of spaghetti on the table.

"Yes," they both replied, looking down.

After that, their mom and dad sat for a long time without talking. All three kids looked back and forth between each other, wondering what was going to happen. When Dad was mad, they knew they had really done it and were in big trouble.

Instead of yelling, Dad quietly spoke to the whole family.

"Paul," Dad started, "I don't like that you are fighting with your siblings. I understand why you are mad, and therefore, I will let this slide." He then looked at Peanut and Scott. "You two need to respect your brother and do not, I repeat, do not use his computer without permission. Do you understand?"

Peanut and Scott nodded their heads up and down.

Then Dad said slowly, "We have come to our decision."

Peanut immediately got butterflies in her stomach. *What was he going to say about the clubhouse?*

"Your mother and I talked about taking the clubhouse away from both of you, but what would that solve?"

"Nothing, Dad," Scott interrupted.

Mom gave Scott a warning look, so he immediately stopped talking.

"As I was saying ..."

Peanut leaned in, wanting to know the answer. But at the same time, she didn't want to know the answer. Would this night ever end?

"Here is the deal," Dad continued. "If you do not figure out a way to work together and share the clubhouse, we will close it permanently. There is no reason why you can't do this."

"What?" both kids said together.

"You have one week to find a way to work this out. End of discussion."

After that, the family ate in silence. No one felt like talking anymore. Peanut just swirled her spaghetti noodles around her plate, thinking how she could possibly share the clubhouse with Scott. Even worse, how would they ever finish their story for the contest with Scott and his friends always around?

★ ☆ ★ ☆ ★ ☆ ★ ☆

Later that night, Peanut made sure she talked to Pinky before she went to sleep. This was serious business, and Peanut needed her best friend more than ever.

"Wow, Peanut," Pinky said into the walkie-talkie. "This is a bummer. A major bummer for us."

"I know. This doesn't seem real. How did this happen?"

"Peanut, we can make this work. We can share the clubhouse," Pinky continued. "It'll be okay. Maybe if

we all try hard, we'll find a way to share and still have a good time."

Although Pinky was trying to be brave for her friend, she didn't really feel that way inside. Pinky worried that Scott would change the clubhouse too much and ruin everything they had worked on.

"I'm sure you're right, Pinky. But the worst part is that if my dad hears us fight at all, he'll shut the clubhouse forever. Forever, Pinky," she said, flopping onto her bed.

"Don't worry. We'll think of something," Pinky said quietly into the walkie-talkie. "Good night, friend."

As Peanut shut off her walkie-talkie, she went to her bedroom window and opened it up. Looking out, she could see their beautiful clubhouse. The girls had had so much fun out there. When she had first found the house while playing ball with Ralphie, it had been covered in icky, sticky spider webs. The windows were covered with dirt so thick she knew a family of ants could've lived in there. The inside was cold and dirty. The girls, with their parents' help, had worked every day in the summer, making it into the most wonderful clubhouse ever. Now all of their hard work was about to be ruined.

"I can't believe it's all over," Peanut said twisting her hair while tears filled her eyes. "How can everything change ... again?"

Chapter 11

Could This Be True?

Was this all a bad dream? Peanut thought to herself as she opened her eyes the next morning. If only she really did have a super power to get speedy-ready for school today.

At the breakfast table, Peanut and Scott just looked at each other. On the bus, they sat on separate sides. They knew if they started fighting, Paul would tell their dad as soon as they got home.

At lunch, Peanut was still feeling miserable.

"Oh, Peanut, maybe it won't be as bad as you think," said Tammy.

"Yeah, remember when my mom was going to have the babies and you told me everything would be okay? Well, this will be okay, too," Pinky said. Of course, Pinky was very nervous about this whole thing, but she couldn't tell that to her best friend right now.

At that moment, Scott walked by and slid Peanut's cookie right off the table, watching it break apart on the lunchroom floor.

"Grow up, Scott," said Peanut.

"*Grow up, Scott*," he said back in a girly voice. "See you in the clubhouse after school, girls. Should be lots of fun."

With that, Scott walked away, laughing loudly.

"Great. How are we going to be in the same clubhouse with him?" asked Peanut "How are we ever going to get our contest story written if he and his friends are in there?"

"I still can't believe this is happening. Do my dad and mom really think Scott and I are going to be able to work this out?"

"Let's go outside and play on the swings. That always helps us feel better," said Tammy.

And that's just what they did.

On the bus ride home, Peanut could hear Scott, cousin Jeff, Mac, and Ethan talking about the clubhouse.

"Yeah, you could even borrow my pet spider for the clubhouse if you want, Scott," said Mac.

"Thanks, man. That's a good idea. I never thought about having a clubhouse pet."

What? A gross spider in the clubhouse? thought Peanut to herself. *Could this get any worse?*

"I'll see you at the clubhouse in an hour," Pinky said, interrupting Peanut's thoughts.

"Okay, I'll see you then. It's your turn to bring the gummi bears, Pinky."

"Okey-doke!"

As Peanut stood up to get off the bus, Scott shouted to his friends, "Be at my house in half an hour. It's clubhouse time."

Peanut still couldn't believe what she was hearing. When she got to her house, she said a quick hello to her mom and went straight to her room. Hopefully, by the time Pinky came over, Scott and his crazy friends would be out of the clubhouse.

She sat on her bed and wondered if they would really be able to figure out a way to share the clubhouse. Maybe Scott just wanted to sit in the clubhouse and read or something. Maybe he and his friends just wanted to use it to rest after playing football. That wouldn't be so bad. The girls would still have all of their things in the clubhouse. Maybe things wouldn't change that much.

Peanut actually felt a teeny tiny bit better. She looked at the clock and realized Pinky would be over any minute.

"I better go to the clubhouse and get our stuff out for the contest before Pinky gets there."

When Peanut opened the clubhouse door, she couldn't believe her eyes. There was Scott, a big hairy spider in a jar, a dirty skateboard, Mac and Ethan, and some boxes lying all over.

"Hey, Peanut. Welcome to my clubhouse. These are my club mates Mac and Ethan."

Peanut stood speechless. Shouldn't he have been gone by now?

"How do you like our new pet? Won't it be fun to let him crawl around?"

All the boys started laughing.

"Scott, that's it! What's all this junk in here for?"

"Junk? This is my stuff. Remember, Peanut, we get to share the clubhouse now. I even have more to bring over. You'll need to get rid of some of your things so I can fit mine."

"SCOTT, I will not!"

"You have to, Peanut."

Just then they heard someone at the door. Oh no, they hoped it wasn't Dad.

"Hey, Peanut Butter, what—" Pinky started, but then she just stood there with her eyes wide open. She hadn't expected to see Scott, his friends, and all their stuff piled in the clubhouse.

"Welcome to my, I mean our, clubhouse, Pinky. Want to see my new pet?"

"Scott, leave me alone."

"Hey, I was just trying to be nice."

"Yeah, right, whatever," said Pinky.

Pinky wanted to stand by her friend, but there wasn't enough room for her.

"Hey, guys, ready to play some football?"

All the guys high-fived each other and left.

Pinky walked in the clubhouse, shutting the door behind her.

"Thank goodness they're out of here," Pinky grumbled.

"So, do you really think everything is going to be fine?"

Pinky didn't say anything. She knew things were changing.

❖❖❖❖❖❖

A few days before, life had been so good. They had found out about the Super Samantha contest, they had gotten the swings three days in a row on the playground, and the clubhouse had been THEIR clubhouse. Now they had boy stuff, a dirty skateboard, and a big black spider in a jar looking at them. If all of these changes happened in one day, what was going to happen next? The girls sat and ate their gummi bears, not wanting to know the answer.

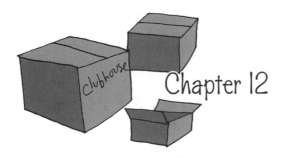

Chapter 12

Feeling Sad

For the next week, Peanut, Pinky, and Tammy found ways of staying out of the clubhouse. Peanut should have been mad at Scott for taking all the fun out of her backyard, but she wasn't. Instead she felt sad; sad that everything had changed. Now her special clubhouse was different, and it just didn't feel the same.

Scott noticed the difference, too. Every time Scott thought Peanut would be at the clubhouse, she wasn't there.

⋆⋅⋆⋅⋆⋅⋆⋅⋆

"Hey, Scott, did you hear anything I said?" Mac repeated to Scott.

"What? No. Um, sorry, Mac," Scott replied.

"Dude, what is going on?" Ethan asked.

"I just have a lot on my mind with school work, which skateboard to ride, walking Ralphie, and ..." Scott couldn't come up with a good excuse for the guys. Why was it bothering him so much seeing Peanut sad? This wasn't the way the clubhouse was supposed to go. *Now what?* Scott thought to himself.

"Oh, hi guys," Peanut said, walking into the clubhouse.

"Hey, Peanut Butter," Scott said. "Are you and your friends coming in here now?"

"No, I just came by to get my bag of gummi bears."

"The guys and I are going to the park to play flag football, so don't go running to Mom and Dad, telling them you didn't get a turn in here today."

"Don't worry about it," Peanut said as she grabbed the gummi bears. She waved goodbye to the boys and left.

"Huh," Mac and Ethan said at the same time.

The boys began talking about other things, but Scott didn't join in. Boy, Peanut looked and sounded sad. Why was she so sad? *Ugghhh*, Scott thought, *now what did I do?*

The next few days were the same for Scott and Peanut. It wasn't fun in the Helfen house, especially for Peanut. Now, only the contest and her friends made her happy. She even told herself she didn't care about having a clubhouse.

"Oh, I'm so nervous!" Tammy said to Pinky and Peanut the next day, standing in front of the mailbox.

"I know, I know!" Pinky said looking at her friends.

They had done it. The girls had finally finished their story for the Super Samantha contest. Now they only had to drop it into the mail slot. But for some reason, the girls just stood there, not moving, afraid to say goodbye to all of their hard work.

"I say, we just drop it in on the count of three," Peanut said, trying to sound like a grownup.

"Oh, Peanut, I'm so nervous!" Tammy said again.

"Okay, everyone, hold onto the package," Pinky said to the others. "One ..."

"Wait, wait, wait!" Tammy interrupted. "Shouldn't we all make a wish before we put it in the mail slot?"

"That's a great idea," Pinky said quickly. "Okay, let's all hold onto the envelope and make a big wish that we win. Deal?"

"Deal!"

Once the wishes were made, the girls counted to three and dropped the envelope into the mail slot.

"All we can do now is wait," Peanut said, looking at the mailbox.

"Well, this is great!" Tammy said cheerfully. "We should be proud of ourselves. I think we'll win."

"Me, too!" Pinky said as she did her favorite ballerina twirl.

As the three girls skipped back to Peanut's back yard, arm in arm, they forgot for a moment about the clubhouse and the fighting. Today they were happier than they had been in a long time. It was sunny out, Ralphie was jumping around, and they had each other as friends.

"Who needs a clubhouse anyway?" Peanut said to Pinky and Tammy, shrugging her shoulders.

As the girls just looked at each other, not saying a word, Peanut thought to herself, *I do*.

Chapter 13

What Was Going On?

"So, my mom said that she will sew some Super Samantha pillow cases for us," Pinky said to Peanut as they were sitting in the clubhouse.

It was one of the few times the girls went to the clubhouse anymore. Scott had left for a basketball tournament earlier that morning, so the girls decided to hang out together while they had the chance.

"Pinky, your mom is so cool and ..." Peanut was about to finish the sentence when the clubhouse door opened, and in walked Scott.

"Hey, girls, whatcha doing?" Scott said with a funny voice. "What'll we do today?" he said, flopping into the beanbag chair.

"Nothing, Scott. We were just leaving," Peanut said, standing up.

"Yeah, no worries, Scott," Pinky chimed in. "Have a great day."

"Why do you always leave when I walk in?" Scott said with a frown. "It's not like I've got cooties."

Scott watched as Pinky leaned over and whispered something to Peanut before she waved goodbye and went out the clubhouse door.

"What was that all about?" Scott said, sounding a little mad.

"Nothing much. Pinky just had to get home."

"Yeah, right," Scott mumbled quietly.

"I want to talk to you, Peanut."

"Okay, Scott, but can you hurry? I don't want to be here when your friends come over."

"They aren't coming over today. I just wanted to hang out with … you this afternoon," Scott said, looking outside the window.

"What?" Peanut couldn't believe what she was hearing. This had to be a joke.

"Scott, you are so mean!"

"What are you talking about, Peanut? I'm serious. I do want to hang out with you."

Peanut STILL couldn't believe this.

She flopped down onto the other beanbag next to Scott, very confused. "You want to hang out with MEEEE?"

"Hey, don't make such a big deal, Peanut Butter."

"But it is a big deal, Scott."

What's going on with Scott? Peanut thought to herself.

"You know, we used to do stuff together at our old place," Scott said.

"Yeah—" Peanut started to say.

"Well, since we moved to Oakdale, we don't anymore," Scott said.

"But I thought you didn't want to play with me."

"Hey, we always used to hang out in Highland, but then you met Pinky here, and that was that."

Peanut wanted to argue, but she knew she couldn't. Scott was right. Funny. She'd never noticed this.

"I'm sorry, Scott."

"That's okay, Peanut. I guess I haven't been very nice to you. I didn't really feel like being nice … I just hated moving. I hated leaving all of my friends. I hated being the new kid in my class."

"You did? You didn't look like you hated it," Peanut said. "You always made fun of me for being so sad."

"I'm not a crybaby like you, Peanut, but—"

"Hey!" Peanut said, standing up, hands on her hips. "I am not a crybaby!"

"I'm sorry," Scott said. "Anyway, I kept trying to get you to hang out, but nooooooo, you were too busy."

"Scott, why didn't you just ask me to hang out?"

"Peanut, come on," Scott said, rolling his eyes. "I don't even really want this clubhouse. It's not that fun. You can have it back," Scott said as he stood up to leave.

"Scott, wait … thanks … no … I mean … you can use the clubhouse, too. I'm sorry. I haven't been very nice, either. I … I didn't mean to chase you out. I can share it with you."

"Really? You wouldn't mind if I was here sometimes?"

"Nope," Peanut said. "Except—"

"Except what?"

"Except you have to get that big, hairy spider out of here!"

Scott and Peanut laughed out loud.

"Okay, Peanut, I guess I can do that."

"Then we can totally hang out, Scott," Peanut said, hugging her brother.

"Hey, hey, Peanut, all right. That's enough," Scott said, taking a step back. "You better not tell anyone about this," Scott said, acting like his old self again.

"Not even Mac and Ethan?" Peanut said, giggling.

"You'll just look crazy 'cause I'll say you're making it up."

With that, Scott left the clubhouse.

Peanut just sat there, wondering if this all had really happened. *Am I dreaming?* she thought. She pinched herself to make sure—*ouch!* Nope, it wasn't a dream. Scott Helfen really did care about his sister.

Chapter 14

Did We Win?

"Okay, are you ready to open the letter?" Peanut said as she held on to the envelope from the Super Samantha contest. She was so excited. The moment the girls had been waiting for was finally here.

"Yes," Pinky and Tammy said together. "But we can't look. Just rip it open and read it."

From closed eyes, Pinky heard Peanut ripping the envelope, unfolding the paper, and then ... nothing. Pinky opened one eye and then the other. She saw Peanut sitting there with a very sad look on her face. Tammy put her arm around her friend.

"We didn't win," Peanut said with tears coming down her face. "What happened?"

"Oh, Peanut," Pinky said, giving her friend a hug, "it's okay."

"I bet they still loved our story," Tammy said with tears falling down her cheeks, too. "It was a great story."

The girls spent a long time just sitting together, not saying much. They were sad, and this would take some time to get over. After what seemed like forever, Pinky wiped the last of her tears away, stood up, and faced the girls, putting her hands on her hips.

"Well, I know why we didn't win," Pinky said in a serious tone.

Peanut and Tammy sat up really straight, waiting for Pinky's answer. Pinky stared at them for a minute, a very quiet minute. She then said in a grownup voice, "The reason we didn't win is because my name wasn't 'Super-fast Girl Who is Quicker Than a Cheetah' like I said I wanted."

Peanut and Tammy just stared at Pinky with funny looks on their faces. Then, all of a sudden, all three girls burst out laughing. They laughed and laughed and hugged each other.

Although they hadn't won the contest, they still had each other.

Chapter 15

The Big Surprise

"Dad, I really thought we'd win," Peanut said at the dinner table. She tried hard not to cry, but she just couldn't stop her tears. Quietly she said, "It was a great story."

"I'm sure it was, Peanut," Dad said. "I bet there were so many wonderful stories like yours that it was hard to choose just one."

"Ashley," her mom added, "aren't you proud of yourself and your friends for all of the hard work you put into your story?"

"Of course, I am, Mom, but I'm still sad."

"I liked your story," Paul said. "It was really good."

"Thank you," Peanut said, trying not to cry again.

Scott just ate his food and didn't say anything.

The rest of the dinner went by slowly for Peanut, and she didn't feel like eating. After everyone was done, she excused herself and went to her room so she could be alone.

"Pinky," Peanut said later into the walkie-talkie, "I just don't feel like talking tonight."

"That's okay, Peanut. I don't either. Good night."

"Good night, Pinky."

Peanut was about to turn off the light when she heard a knock on her door. "I don't want to talk right now," she said.

"Peanut, can I come in for a minute?" Scott said, peeking his head in the doorway.

"Oh, fine," Peanut said, rolling her eyes. "I'm really tired so could you make it quick?"

"Here." Scott pulled something from behind his back and tossed it on her lap and left quickly.

What is this? Peanut thought as she looked at the envelope Scott had given her. As she opened the letter, her eyes opened wide. In big red letters, the word "WINNER" stared at her. But this was not her story. It was … Scott's! Scott's? Peanut jumped up from her bed and ran to Scott's room as fast as she could.

"Scott, Scott, what is this?" Peanut said, bursting into his room.

"It's nothing, Peanut. I just wanted to show it to you."

"You won the contest?"

"Hey, don't make such a big deal. I was bored so I entered."

"Scott, I thought it wasn't cool enough for you," Peanut said, flopping down onto his bed.

"Yeah, but ...," he said, sitting down next to her, "you all talked so much about it that I just started getting ideas on what to write."

Peanut looked at the title of Scott's story, *The Amazing Ashley and Her Brave Brother Super Scott*. Peanut looked up at her brother. "You wrote a story about us? How did you know this was the name I wanted?"

"Oh, I heard you talking with your friends one day. You know you guys are just soooo loud."

"Can I read it?"

"Yeah, it's for you, Peanut."

"Oh, wow, Scott. Thank you," Peanut said, giving her brother a hug.

And this time, Scott hugged her back. All day, he hadn't said a word about winning. But now that he saw Peanut felt okay with it, he could finally show how happy he felt.

Peanut hadn't won, but she just beamed with pride for her brother and kept hugging him.

As Peanut began to leave with Scott's story in her hand, he stopped her.

"Hey, Peanut, I want you to stand next to me at the assembly when Super Samantha and Amazing Jake come to our school. Okay?" Scott said quietly.

Before Peanut could hug her brother again, he said, "All right, all right, that's enough. I'm going to bed now, so buzz off."

Peanut just smiled and skipped back to her room.

Chapter 16

Can This Really Be Happening?

"Wow!" Peanut said to herself as she looked at all the kids sitting in the gym. "Can this really be happening?"

Peanut, Scott, and Mr. McPatrick were standing in front of all the students of Oakdale Elementary. The crowd was talking with excitement, waiting for the super-heroes to arrive. The Oakdale band was playing in the back, Mrs. Staiger, the vice-principal, was making sure the microphone worked, and bunches of red and blue balloons (Super Samantha and Amazing Jake's favorite colors) hung in the air everywhere.

Principal McPatrick leaned over and said, "Super Samantha and Amazing Jake should be here any minute. Are you ready?"

Both Peanut and Scott shook their heads and smiled at each other. Peanut thought that even Mr. McPatrick looked excited.

Peanut was about to pinch herself again to make sure this wasn't a dream. She remembered, though, how much it hurt the last time she did that. So, she gave Scott a quick pinch instead.

"Ow! What did you do that for?" Scott asked.

"Sorry, I just wanted to make sure I wasn't dreaming."

"Whatever, geez," Scott said, rolling his eyes.

Mr. McPatrick took the microphone and quieted all the students down. He talked about Scott's story, how proud he was of all the students at the school, and how honored they should be to have the super heroes visit them.

Then all of a sudden, a loud boom exploded, and Super Samantha and Amazing Jake came running into the gym. (Even though the students weren't supposed to run, Principal McPatrick had made an exception for the two that day.) Everyone stood up, clapped their hands, and shouted with excitement. The band banged on the drums. And even the teachers had great big grins on their faces. Peanut would never forget that moment.

"Peanut, I can't believe you got to meet Super Samantha," Tammy said.

"Oh my gosh, I couldn't even sit still. I wanted to clap, laugh, and do a ballerina spin all at the same time," Pinky shouted.

"I still can't believe it. I actually got hugs from both of them. They were soooo nice—and funny, too," Peanut said. "Can you believe they put those special wires on Scott and had him flying through the gym? Boy, that was awesome."

The bus ride home was unusually loud. All the kids were talking about the super heroes' visit. And everyone was asking Scott tons of questions. He was loving every minute of it ... even though he would never admit it.

"Bye, Tammy. I'll see you later."

"Okay. Bye, Peanut."

The bus pulled up in front of Peanut's house next. The kids on the bus cheered as Scott and Peanut stood up.

"Hey, dude, awesome time at school today," shouted Mac.

"Yeah, way cool," said Ethan. "See you later. I'll ride my bike over."

"Hey, Peanut, I'm going to finish my homework, and then I'll be over." Pinky then leaned towards Peanut and whispered, "Any chance those boys won't be in the clubhouse today?"

"Don't worry, Pinky. We'll be fine." Peanut then looked at Scott and gave him a grin.

Chapter 17

A New Adventure for Everyone

"Pass the gummi bears, Peanut," Pinky said as she pulled the journal out from their secret hiding place.

"Here you go."

"All right, we have got to draw the coolest picture of Super Samantha," Peanut said in excitement.

The girls were so involved with their picture that they didn't hear the clubhouse door open.

"Hey, girls!"

"AHHHHH!" They knew who it was without even looking.

"Give us a minute, Scott, pleeeassse," Pinky said. "We're almost done."

"I just wanted to know if you guys want to play kickball at the park on the other side of school. Mom said it was okay since Mac's mom will be there. So, go get your bikes."

Pinky stood there for a moment, smiled, and rushed out of the clubhouse without a word. Peanut just hoped that Pinky was running to get her bike and not running away from Scott.

"Well, I guess we're done *now*," Peanut said, rolling her eyes at Scott.

After putting the journal away, they headed out, grabbed their bikes, and went to meet up with Pinky and Ethan and ride to the park.

"Hey, I've never been to this park before. I hope they have monkey bars because I love to climb them. And swings, ones with long chains so you can go way high up. Wouldn't that be great?" Pinky said.

But when the kids reached the edge of the park, they all stopped and just looked around.

"This … is the park?" Pinky said.

"Why is garbage all over the ground?" Peanut said, looking around.

"Man, this is bad," Ethan said.

"No wonder nobody talks about this park," said Scott.

As the kids looked around, they saw broken soda bottles on the ground, words and pictures spray-painted

on the fence, and a baseball field full of weeds, overgrown grass, and dirt holes.

"My mom's in the car, and she said we can't play here," Mac said. "As if we'd want to, huh? Wow, this place is really dirty. Look at the broken slide, and the swing set doesn't have any swings."

"All right guys, let's leave. Let's go back to our house and play kickball," Scott said to the group.

As the boys rode ahead, Pinky and Peanut slowly got back on their bikes and looked at the park for a minute.

"Pinky, what does that say over there?"

On one of the fences at the park, a sign said, "PLEASE SAVE OUR PARK. HOW WILL YOU HELP?"

"Do you think we could do anything, Peanut? We're only eight."

"Yeah, we're only eight, but we know a lot of people. And look what we did with our clubhouse."

"It was really bad when you found it," Pinky said wrinkling her nose.

"What if we thought of the park as a GIANT clubhouse?"

"We're going to need a lot more help," Pinky said.

"Let's talk tonight on the walkie-talkies. I'll get our journal, and we'll make a list."

"Okay, but right now, let's go play kickball with the guys, Pinky. Is that okay?"

"Yeah, of course. It's going to be fun."

The girls rode back to Peanut's house without saying a word, their heads filled with all that had happened that day. They knew their biggest adventure was about to begin. But for now, they all would just play together. Tomorrow, they would think about the park.

Deena (Cloutier) Cook is enjoying her adventure as a writer. She currently resides in the beautiful Pacific Northwest with her husband and three children. Writing is a dream come true and each day is a wonderful adventure. She looks forward to sharing many new stories with the readers.

Cherie (Helfen) McIntosh is an author of fiction stories for children. She feels honored to share her passion of writing stories with young children. She is a former elementary teacher. Originally from Indiana, she currently lives in the Pacific Northwest with her husband and two children.

Trina (Sullivan) Scruggs has always enjoyed drawing cartoons and has been drawing since she was 2 years old. She enjoys all different kinds of art and works mostly from her studio in Bellevue, Washington. She loves spending time with her family, her husband, her son and her four poodles.

We hope you enjoyed
Pinky and Peanut: No Boys Allowed
Pinky and Peanut would like to hear from you.

Visit the girls at:
www.pinkyandpeanut.com

Or

Write to them at:

4957 Lakemont Blvd. SE

STE C-4 #316

Bellevue, WA 98006